Thomas Bailey Aldrich

XXXVI Lyrics and XII Sonnets

Thomas Bailey Aldrich

XXXVI Lyrics and XII Sonnets

ISBN/EAN: 9783744768993

Printed in Europe, USA, Canada, Australia, Japan

Cover: Foto ©Andreas Hilbeck / pixelio.de

More available books at **www.hansebooks.com**

T. B. ALDRICH

XXXVI Lyrics
and XII Sonnets

SELECTED FROM

CLOTH OF GOLD
AND
FLOWER AND THORN

BOSTON
HOUGHTON, MIFFLIN AND COMPANY
The Riverside Press, Cambridge
1881

The Riverside Press, Cambridge:
Electrotyped and Printed by H. O. Houghton & Co.

TO L. A.

Take them and keep them,
Silvery thorn and flower,
Plucked just at random
In the rosy weather —
Snowdrops and pansies,
Sprigs of wayside heather,
And five-leaved wild-rose
Dead within an hour.

Take them and keep them :
Who can tell? some day, dear,
(Though they be withered,
Flower and thorn and blossom,)
Held for an instant
Up against thy bosom,
They might make December
Seem to thee like May, dear!

CONTENTS.

LYRICS.

I.

DESTINY.

Three roses, wan as moonlight and
    weighed down
Each with its loveliness as with a crown,
Drooped in a florist's window in a town.

The first a lover bought. It lay at rest,
Like flower on flower, that night, on
    Beauty's breast.

The second rose, as virginal and fair,
Shrunk in the tangles of a harlot's hair.

The third, a widow, with new grief made
    wild, ·
Shut in the icy palm of her dead child.

II.

HESPERIDES.

If thy soul, Herrick, dwelt with me,
This is what my songs would be :
Hints of our sea-breezes, blent
With odors from the Orient ;
Indian vessels deep with spice ;
Star-showers from the Norland ice ;
Wine-red jewels that seem to hold
Fire, but only burn with cold ;
Antique goblets, strangely wrought,
Filled with the wine of happy thought ;
Bridal measures, vain regrets,
Laburnum buds and violets ;
Hopeful as the break of day ;
Clear as crystal ; new as May ;
Musical as brooks that run
O'er yellow shallows in the sun ;
Soft as the satin fringe that shades
The eyelids of thy fragrant maids ;
Brief as thy lyrics, Herrick, are,
And polished as the bosom of a star.

III.

IDENTITY.

Somewhere — in desolate wind-swept
    space —
In Twilight-land—in No-man's-land—
Two hurrying Shapes met face to face,
    And bade each other stand.

"And who are you?" cried one, agape,
    Shuddering in the gloaming light.
"I know not," said the second Shape,
    "I only died last night!"

IV.

NOCTURNE.

BELLAGGIO.

Up to her chamber window
A slight wire trellis goes,
And up this Romeo's ladder
Clambers a bold white rose.

I lounge in the ilex shadows,
I see the lady lean,
Unclasping her silken girdle,
The curtain's folds between.

She smiles on her white-rose lover,
She reaches out her hand
And helps him in at the window —
I see it where I stand !

To her scarlet lip she holds him,
And kisses him many a time —
Ah, me ! it was he that won her
Because he dared to climb !

V.

THE SHEIK'S WELCOME.

Because thou com'st, a weary guest,
Unto my tent, I bid thee rest.
This cruse of oil, this skin of wine,
These tamarinds and dates, are thine;
And whilst thou eatest, Medjid, there,
Shall bathe the heated nostrils of thy
    mare.

Allah il' Allah !   Even so
An Arab chieftain treats a foe,
Hold him as one without a fault
Who breaks his bread and tastes his
    salt ;
And, in fair battle, strikes him dead
With the same pleasure that he gives
    him bread !

VI.

PALABRAS CARIÑOSAS.

SPANISH AIR.

Good-night! I have to say good-night
To such a host of peerless things!
Good-night unto that fragile hand
All queenly with its weight of rings;
Good-night to fond, uplifted eyes,
Good-night to chestnut braids of hair,
Good-night unto the perfect mouth,
And all the sweetness nestled there —
　　The snowy hand detains me, then
　　I 'll have to say good-night again!

But there will come a time, my love,
When, if I read our stars aright,
I shall not linger by this porch
With my adieus. Till then, good-night!
You wish the time were now? And I.
You do not blush to wish it so?
You would have blushed yourself to
　　death

To own so much a year ago —
  What, both these snowy hands ! ah,
    then,
  I 'll have to say good-night again !
    2

VII.

A SNOW-FLAKE.

Once he sang of summer,
Nothing but the summer ;
Now he sings of winter,
Of winter bleak and drear :
Just because there 's fallen
A snow-flake on his forehead,
He must go and fancy
'T is winter all the year !

VIII.

ACROSS THE STREET.

With lash on cheek, she comes and
    goes ;
I watch her when she little knows :
  I wonder if she dreams of it.
Sitting and working at my rhymes,
I weave into my verse at times
  Her sunny hair, or gleams of it.

Upon her window-ledge is set
A box of flowering mignonette ;
  Morning and eve she tends to them —
The senseless flowers, that do not care
About that loosened strand of hair,
  As prettily she bends to them.

If I could once contrive to get
Into that box of mignonette
  Some morning when she tends to
    them —
She comes !   I see the rich blood rise
From throat to cheek ! — down go the
    eyes,
  Demurely, as she bends to them !

,

IX.

RENCONTRE.

Toiling across the Mer de Glace,
I thought of, longed for thee ;
What miles between us stretched, alas !
What miles of land and sea !

My foe, undreamed of, at my side
Stood suddenly, like Fate.
For those who love, the world is wide,
But not for those who hate.

X.

AN UNTIMELY THOUGHT.

I wonder what day of the week —
I wonder what month of the year —
Will it be midnight, or morning,
And who will bend over my bier?

— What a hideous fancy to come
As I wait, at the foot of the stair,
While Lilian gives the last touch
To her robe, or the rose in her hair.

Do I like your new dress — pompadour?
And do I like *you?*   On my life,
You are eighteen, and not a day more,
And have not been six years my wife.

Those two rosy boys in the crib
Up stairs are not ours, to be sure ! —
You are just a sweet bride in her bloom,
All sunshine, and snowy, and pure.

As the carriage rolls down the dark
  street
The little wife laughs and makes cheer ;
But . . . I wonder what day of the
  week,
I wonder what month of the year.

XI.

NAMELESS PAIN.

In my nostrils the summer wind
Blows the exquisite scent of the rose !
O for the golden, golden wind,
Breaking the buds as it goes,
Breaking the buds, and bending the
grass,
And spilling the scent of the rose !

O wind of the summer morn,
Tearing the petals in twain,
Wafting the fragrant soul
Of the rose through valley and plain,
I would you could tear my heart to-day,
And scatter its nameless pain.

XII.

ON AN INTAGLIO HEAD OF MINERVA.

Beneath the warrior's helm, behold
The flowing tresses of the woman !
Minerva, Pallas, what you will —
A winsome creature, Greek or Roman.

Minerva ?   No, 't is some sly minx
In cousin's helmet masquerading ;
If not — then Wisdom was a dame
For sonnets and for serenading !

I thought the goddess cold, austere,
Not   made   for   love's   despairs   and
        blisses :
Did Pallas wear her hair like that ?
Was   Wisdom's   mouth   so   shaped   for
        kisses ?

The Nightingale should be her bird,
And not the Owl, big-eyed and solemn :
How very fresh she looks, and yet
She 's older far than Trajan's Column !

The magic hand that carved this face,
And set this vine-work round it running,
Perhaps ere mighty Phidias wrought
Had lost its subtle skill and cunning.

Who was he ?   Was he glad or sad,
Who knew to carve in such a fashion ?
Perchance he graved the dainty head
For some brown girl that scorned his
    passion.

Perchance, in some still garden-place,
Where neither fount nor tree to-day is,
He flung the jewel at the feet
Of Phryne, or perhaps 't was Laïs.

But he is dust ; we may not know
His happy or unhappy story :
Nameless, and dead these centuries,
His work outlives him — there 's his
    glory !

Both man and jewel lay in earth
Beneath a lava-buried city ;
The countless summers came and went
With neither haste, nor hate, nor pity.

Years blotted out the man, but left
The jewel fresh as any blossom,
Till some Visconti dug it up —
To rise and fall on Mabel's bosom !

O nameless brother ! see how Time
Your gracious handiwork has guarded :
See how your loving, patient art
Has come, at last, to be rewarded.

Who would not suffer slights of men,
And pangs of hopeless passion also,
To have his carven agate-stone
On such a bosom rise and fall so!

ι

XIII.

THE ONE WHITE ROSE.

A sorrowful woman said to me,
" Come in and look on our child."
I saw an Angel at shut of day,
And it never spoke — but smiled.

I think of it in the city's streets,
I dream of it when I rest —
The violet eyes, the waxen hands,
And the one white rose on the breast !

．

XIV.

THE QUEEN'S RIDE.

AN INVITATION.

'T is that fair time of year,
　　　Lady mine,
When stately Guinevere,
In her sea-green robe and hood,
Went a-riding through the wood,
　　　Lady mine.

And as the Queen did ride,
　　　Lady mine,
Sir Launcelot at her side
Laughed and chatted, bending over,
Half her friend and all her lover!
　　　Lady mine.

And as they rode along,
　　　Lady mine,
The throstle gave them song,
And the buds peeped through the grass
To see youth and beauty pass !
　　　Lady mine.

And on, through deathless time,
     Lady mine,
These lovers in their prime,
(Two fairy ghosts together !)
Ride, with sea-green robe, and feather !
     Lady mine.

And so we two will ride,
     Lady mine,
At your pleasure, side by side,
Laugh and chat ; I bending over,
Half your friend and all your lover !
     Lady mine.

But if you like not this,
     Lady mine,
And take my love amiss,
Then I 'll ride unto the end,
Half your lover, all your friend !
     Lady mine.

So, come which way you will,
     Lady mine,
Vale, upland, plain, and hill
Wait your coming. For one day
Loose the bridle, and away !
     Lady mine.

XV.

ROCOCO.

By studying my lady's eyes
I 've grown so learnèd day by day,
So Machiavelian in this wise,
That when I send her flowers, I say

To each small flower (no matter what,
Geranium, pink, or tuberose,
Syringa, or forget-me-not,
Or violet) before it goes :

" Be not triumphant, little flower,
When on her haughty heart you lie,
But modestly enjoy your hour :
She 'll weary of you by and by."

XVI.

DIRGE.

Let us keep him warm,
Stir the dying fire :
Upon his tired arm
Slumbers young Desire.

Soon, ah, very soon
We too shall not know
Either sun or moon,
Either grass or snow.

Others in our place
Come to laugh and weep,
Win or lose the race,
And to fall asleep.

Let us keep him warm,
Stir the dying fire :
Upon his tired arm
Slumbers young Desire.

What does all avail —
Love, or power, or gold ?
Life is like a tale
Ended ere 't is told.

Much is left unsaid,
Much is said in vain —
Shall the broken thread
Be taken up again ?

Let us keep him warm,
Stir the dying fire :
Upon his tired arm
Slumbers young Desire.

Kisses one or two
On his eyelids set,
That, when all is through,
He may not forget.

He has far to go —
Is it East or West ?
Whither ?   Who may know !
Let him take his rest.

Wind, and snow, and sleet —
So the long night dies.

Draw the winding-sheet,
Cover up his eyes.

Let us keep him warm,
Stir the dying fire :
Upon his tired arm
Slumbers young Desire.

XVII.

BEFORE THE RAIN.

We knew it would rain, for all the
　　morn,
A spirit on slender ropes of mist
Was lowering its golden buckets down
Into the vapory amethyst

Of marshes and swamps and dismal
　　fens —
Scooping the dew that lay in the flowers,
Dipping the jewels out of the sea,
To sprinkle them over the land in
　　showers.

We knew it would rain, for the poplars
　　showed
The white of their leaves, the amber
　　grain
Shrunk in the wind — and the lightning
　　now
Is tangled in tremulous skeins of rain !

XVIII.

AFTER THE RAIN.

The rain has ceased, and in my room
The sunshine pours an airy flood ;
And on the church's dizzy vane
The ancient Cross is bathed in blood.

From out the dripping ivy-leaves,
Antiquely-carven, gray and high,
A dormer, facing westward, looks
Upon the village like an eye :

And now it glimmers in the sun,
A globe of gold, a disc, a speck :
And in the belfry sits a Dove
With purple ripples on her neck.

XIX.

THE UNFORGIVEN.

Near my bed, there, hangs the picture
    jewels could not buy from me :
'T is a Siren, a brown Siren, in her sea-
    weed drapery,
Playing on a lute of amber, by the
    margin of a sea.

In the east, the rose of morning seems
    as if 't would blossom soon,
But it never, never blossoms, in this
    picture; and the moon
Never ceases to be crescent, and the
    June is always June !

And the heavy-branched banana never
    yields its creamy fruit ;
In the citron-trees are nightingales
    forever stricken mute ;
And the Siren sits, her fingers on the
    pulses of the lute.

In the hushes of the midnight, when the
    heliotropes grow strong
With the dampness, I hear music —
    hear a quiet, plaintive song —
A most sad, melodious utterance, as of
    some immortal wrong —

Like the pleading, oft repeated, of a
    Soul that pleads in vain,
Of a damnèd Soul repentant, that would
    fain be pure again ! —
And I lie awake and listen to the music
    of her pain !

And whence comes this mournful music ?
    — whence, unless it chance to be
From the Siren, the brown Siren, in her
    sea-weed drapery,
Playing on a lute of amber, by the
    margin of a sea !

xx.

LOVE'S CALENDAR.

The Summer comes and the Summer
    goes ;
Wild-flowers are fringing the dusty
    lanes,
The swallows go darting through fra-
    grant rains,
Then, all of a sudden — it snows.

Dear Heart, our lives so happily flow,
So lightly we heed the flying hours,
We only know Winter is gone — by the
    flowers,
We only know Winter is come — by the
    snow.

XXI.

LATAKIA.

When all the panes are hung with frost,
Wild wizard-work of silver lace,
I draw my sofa on the rug
Before the ancient chimney-place.
Upon the painted tiles are mosques
And minarets, and here and there
A blind muezzin lifts his hands
And calls the faithful unto prayer.
Folded in idle, twilight dreams,
I hear the hemlock chirp and sing
As if within its ruddy core
It held the happy heart of Spring.
Ferdousi never sang like that,
Nor Saadi grave, nor Hafiz gay:
I lounge, and blow white rings of
      smoke,
And watch them rise and float away.

The curling wreaths like turbans seem
Of silent slaves that come and go —

Or Viziers, packed with craft and crime,
Whom I behead from time to time,
With pipe-stem, at a single blow.

And now and then a lingering cloud
Takes gracious form at my desire,
And at my side my lady stands,
Unwinds her veil with snowy hands —
A shadowy shape, a breath of fire !

O Love, if you were only here
Beside me in this mellow light,
Though all the bitter winds should blow,
And all the ways be choked with snow,
'T would be a true Arabian night !

XXII.

A WINTER-PIECE.

Sous le voile qui vous protége,
Défiant les regards jaloux,
Si vous sortez par cette neige,
Redoutez vos pieds andalous.
                    THÉOPHILE GAUTIER.

Beneath the heavy veil you wear,
Shielded from jealous eyes you go ;
But of your pretty feet have care
If you should venture through the snow.

Howe'er you tread, a dainty mould
Betrays that light foot all the same ;
Upon this glistening snowy fold
At every step it signs your name.

Thus guided, one might come too close
Upon the slyly-hidden nest
Where Psyche, with her cheek's cold
        rose,
On Love's warm bosom lies at rest.

XXIII.

TIGER LILIES.

I like not lady-slippers,
Nor yet the sweet-pea blossoms,
Not yet the flaky roses,
    Red, or white as snow;
I like the chaliced lilies,
The heavy Eastern lilies,
The gorgeous tiger-lilies,
    That in our garden grow !

For they are tall and slender;
Their mouths are dashed with carmine,
And when the wind sweeps by them,
    On their emerald stalks
They bend so proud and graceful —
They are Circassian women,
The favorites of the Sultan,
    Adown our garden walks !

And when the rain is falling,
I sit beside the window
And watch them glow and glisten,
    How they burn and glow !

O for the burning lilies,
The tender Eastern lilies,
The gorgeous tiger-lilies,
    That in our garden grow !

XXIV.

PISCATAQUA RIVER.

Thou singest by the gleaming isles,
By woods and fields of corn,
Thou singest, and the heaven smiles
Upon my birthday morn.

But I within a city, I,
So full of vague unrest,
Would almost give my life to lie
An hour upon thy breast;

To let the wherry listless go,
And, wrapt in dreamy joy,
Dip, and surge idly to and fro,
Like the red harbor-buoy !

To sit in happy indolence,
To rest upon the oars,
And catch the heavy earthy scents
That blow from summer shores :

To see the rounded sun go down,
And with its parting fires

Light up the windows of the town
And burn the tapering spires :

And then to hear the muffled tolls
From steeples slim and white,
And watch, among the Isles of Shoals,
The Beacon's orange light.

O River ! flowing to the main
Through woods and fields of corn,
Hear thou my longing and my pain
This sunny birthday morn :

And take this song which sorrow shapes
To music like thine own,
And sing it to the cliffs and capes
And crags where I am known !

XXV.

QUATRAINS.

Masks.

Black Tragedy lets slip her grim dis-
    guise
And shows you laughing lips and roguish
    eyes ;
But when, unmasked, gay Comedy ap-
    pears,
How wan her cheeks are, and what heavy
    tears !

The Rose.

Fixed to her necklace, like another gem,
A rose she wore — the flower June made
    for her :
Fairer it looked than when upon the
    stem,
And must, indeed, have been much hap-
    pier.

The Parcæ.

In their dark House of Cloud
The three weird sisters toil till time be
    sped ;

One unwinds life ; one ever weaves the
    shroud ;
  One waits to cut the thread.

Grace and Strength.

Manoah's son, in his blind rage malign
Tumbling the temple down upon his foes,
Did no such feat as yonder delicate vine
That day by day untired holds up a rose.

Popularity.

Such kings of shreds have wooed and
    won her,
  Such crafty knaves her laurel owned,
It has become almost an honor
    Not to be crowned.

Maple Leaves.

October turned my maple's leaves to
    gold ;
The most are gone now ; here and there
    one lingers :
Soon these will slip from out the twigs'
    weak hold,
Like coins between a dying miser's fin-
    gers.

XXVI.

LAMIA.

"Go on your way, and let me pass.
You stop a wild despair.
I would that I were turned to brass
Like that chained lion there,

"Which, couchant by the postern gate,
In weather foul or fair,
Looks down serenely desolate,
And nothing does but stare !

"Ah, what's to me the burgeoned year,
The sad leaf or the gay ?
Let Launcelot and Queen Guinevere
Their falcons fly this day.

"'T will be as royal sport, pardie,
As falconers have tried
At Astolat — but let me be !
I would that I had died.

"I met a woman in the glade :
Her hair was soft and brown,

And long bent silken lashes weighed
Her ivory eyelids down.

" I kissed her hand, I called her blest,
I held her leal and fair —
She turned to shadow on my breast,
And melted in the air !

" And, lo ! about me, fold on fold,
A writhing serpent hung —
An eye of jet, a skin of gold,
A garnet for a tongue !

" O, let the petted falcons fly
Right merry in the sun ;
But let me be ! for I shall die
Before the year is done."

XXVII.

AMONTILLADO.

VINTAGE, 1826.

Rafters black with smoke,
White with sand the floor is,
Twenty whiskered Dons
Calling to Dolores —
Tawny flower of Spain,
Wild-rose of Granada,
Keeper of the wines
In this old posada.

Hither, light-of-foot,
Dolores, Hebe, Circe ! —
Pretty Spanish girl,
With not a bit of mercy !
Here I 'm sad and sick,
Faint and thirsty very,
And she does n't bring
The Amontillado Sherry !

Thank you.   Breath of June !
Now my heart beats free, ah !

Kisses for your hand,
Amigita mia !
You shall live in song,
Ripe and warm and cheery,
Mellowing with years,
Like Amontillado Sherry.

Evil spirits, fly !
Care, begone, blue dragon !
Only shapes of joy
Are sculptured on the flagon :
Lyrics — repartees —
Kisses — all that 's merry,
Rise to touch the lip
In Amontillado Sherry !

Here be worth and wealth,
And love, the arch enchanter ;
Here the golden blood
Of saints in this decanter !
When old Charon comes
To row me o'er his ferry,
I 'll bribe him with a case
Of Amontillado Sherry !

While the earth spins round
And the stars lean over,

May this amber sprite
Never lack a lover.
Blessèd be the man
Who lured her from the berry,
And blest the girl who brings
The Amontillado Sherry.

What ! the flagon 's dry ?
Hark, old Time's confession —
Both hands crost at XII,
Owning his transgression !
Pray, old monk ! for all
Generous souls and merry,
May they have their fill
Of Amontillado Sherry !

XXVIII.

THE FADED VIOLET.

What thought is folded in thy leaves !
What tender thought, what speechless
     pain !
I hold thy faded lips to mine,
Thou darling of the April rain !

I hold thy faded lips to mine,
Though scent and azure tint are fled —
O dry, mute lips ! ye are the type
Of something in me cold and dead :

Of something wilted like thy leaves ;
Of fragrance flown, of beauty dim ;
Yet, for the love of those white hands
That found thee by a river's brim —

That found thee when thy dewy mouth
Was purpled as with stains of wine —
For love of her who love forgot,
I hold thy faded lips to mine.

That thou shouldst live when I am dead,
When hate is dead, for me, and wrong,
For this, I use my subtlest art,
For this, I fold thee in my song.

XXIX.

"AH SAD ARE THEY WHO KNOW NOT LOVE."

Ah, sad are they who know not love,
But, far from passion's tears and smiles,
Drift down a moonless sea, beyond
The silvery coasts of fairy isles.

And sadder they whose longing lips
Kiss empty air, and never touch
The dear warm mouth of those they
    love —
Waiting, wasting, suffering much.

But clear as amber, fine as musk,
Is life to those who, pilgrim-wise,
Move hand in hand from dawn to dusk,
Each morning nearer Paradise.

O, not for them shall angels pray!
They stand in everlasting light,
They walk in Allah's smile by day,
And nestle in his heart by night.

XXX.

THE KING'S WINE.

The small green grapes in countless
    clusters grew,
Feeding on mystic moonlight and white
    dew,
And mellow sunshine, the long summer
    through :

Till, with faint tremor in her veins, the
    Vine
Felt the delicious pulses of the wine ;
And the grapes ripened in the year's
    decline.

And day by day the Virgins watched
    their charge ;
And when, at last, beyond the horizon's
    marge,
The harvest-moon droopt beautiful and
    large,

The subtile spirit in the grape was
    caught,
And to the. slowly-dying Monarch
    brought
In a great cup fantastically wrought.

Of this he drank ; then straightway
    from his brain
Went the weird malady, and once again
He walked the Palace, free of scar or
    pain —

But strangely changed, for somehow he
    had lost
Body and voice : the courtiers, as he
    crossed
The royal chambers, whispered — *The
    King's ghost !*

XXXI.

CASTLES.

There is a picture in my brain
That only fades to come again —
The sunlight, through a veil of rain
　　　　To leeward, gilding
A narrow stretch of brown sea-sand,
A light-house half a league from land,
And two young lovers, hand in hand,
　　　　A castle-building.

Upon the budded apple-trees
The robins sing by twos and threes,
And ever at the faintest breeze
　　　　Down drops a blossom ;
And ever would that lover be
The wind that robs the burgeoned tree,
And lifts the soft tress daintily
　　　　On Beauty's bosom.

Ah, graybeard, what a happy thing
It was, when life was in its spring,
To peep through love's betrothal ring
　　　　At Fields Elysian,

To move and breathe in magic air,
To think that all that seems is fair —
Ah, ripe young mouth and golden hair,
    Thou pretty vision !

Well, well, I think not on these two
But the old wound breaks out anew,
And the old dream, as if 't were true,
    In my heart nestles ;
Then tears come welling to my eyes,
For yonder, all in saintly guise,
As 't were, a sweet dead woman lies
    Upon the trestles !

XXXII.

UNSUNG.

As sweet as the breath that goes
From the lips of the white rose,
As weird as the elfin lights
That glimmer of frosty nights,
As wild as the winds that tear
The curled red leaf in the air,
Is the song I have never sung.

In slumber, a hundred times
I have said the mystic rhymes,
But ere I open my eyes
This ghost of a poem flies;
Of the interfluent strains
Not even a note remains :
I know by my pulses' beat
It was something wild and sweet,
And my heart is strangely stirred
By an unremembered word !

I strive, but I strive in vain,
To recall the lost refrain.

On some miraculous day
Perhaps it will come and stay;
In some unimagined Spring
I may find my voice, and sing
The song I have never sung.

XXXIII.

AN OLD CASTLE.

The gray arch crumbles,
And totters, and tumbles ;
The bat has built in the banquet hall :
In the donjon-keep
Sly mosses creep ;
The ivy has scaled the southern wall.
No man-at-arms
Sounds quick alarms
A-top of the cracked martello tower ;
The drawbridge-chain
Is broken in twain —
The bridge will neither rise nor lower.
Not any manner
Of broidered banner
Flaunts at a blazoned herald's call.
Lilies float
In the stagnant moat ;
And fair they are, and tall.

Here, in the old
Forgotten springs,

Was wassail held by queens and kings ;
Here at the board
Sat clown and lord,
Maiden fair and lover bold,
Baron fat and minstrel lean,
The prince with his stars,
The knight with his scars,
The priest in his gabardine.

Where is she
Of the fleur-de-lys,
And that true knight who wore her
      gages ?
Where are the glances
That bred wild fancies
In curly heads of my lady's pages ?
Where are those
Who, in steel or hose,
Held revel here, and made them gay ?
Where is the laughter
That shook the rafter —
Where is the rafter, by the way ?
Gone is the roof,
And perched aloof
Is an owl, like a friar of Orders Gray.
(Perhaps 't is the priest
Come back to feast—

He had ever a tooth for capon, he!
But the capon's cold,
And the steward's old,
And the butler's lost the larder-key!)

The doughty lords
Sleep the sleep of swords.
Dead are the dames and damozels.
The King in his crown
Hath laid him down,
And the Jester with his bells.

All is dead here:
Poppies are red here,
Vines in my lady's chamber grow —
If 't was her chamber
Where they clamber
Up from the poisonous weeds below.
All is dead here,
Joy is fled here;
Let us hence.   'T is the end of all —
The gray arch crumbles,
And totters, and tumbles,
And Silence sits in the banquet hall.

XXXIV.

THE FLIGHT OF THE GODDESS.

A man should live in a garret aloof,
And have few friends, and go poorly
    clad,
With an old hat stopping the chink in
    the roof,
To keep the Goddess constant and glad.

Of old, when I walked on a rugged way,
And gave much work for but little
    bread,
The Goddess dwelt with me night and
    day,
Sat at my table, haunted my bed.

The narrow, mean attic, I see it now! —
Its window o'erlooking the city's tiles,
The sunset's fires, and the clouds of
    snow,
And the river wandering miles and
    miles.

5

Just one picture hung in the room,
The saddest story that Art can tell —
Dante and Virgil in lurid gloom
Watching the Lovers float through Hell.

Wretched enough was I sometimes,
Pinched, and harassed with vain de-
    sires ;
But thicker than clover sprung the
    rhymes
As I dwelt like a sparrow among the
    spires.

Midnight filled my slumbers with song;
Music haunted my dreams by day :
Now I listen and wait and long,
But the Delphian airs have died away.

I wonder and wonder how it befell :
Suddenly I had friends in crowds ;
I bade the house-tops a long farewell;
" Good by," I cried, " to the stars and
    clouds !

" But thou, rare soul, that hast dwelt
    with me,
Spirit of Poesy ! thou divine

Breath of the morning, thou shalt be,
Goddess! for ever and ever mine."

And the woman I loved was now my
    bride,
And the house I wanted was my own;
I turned to the Goddess satisfied —
But the Goddess had somehow flown!

Flown, and I fear she will never return:
I am much too sleek and happy for her,
Whose lovers must hunger, and waste,
    and burn,
Ere the beautiful heathen heart will stir.

I call — but she does not stoop to my
    cry;
I wait — but she lingers, and ah! so
    long!
It was not so in the years gone by,
When she touched my lips with chrism
    of song.

I swear I will get me a garret again,
And adore, like a Parsee, the sunset's
    fires,
And lure the Goddess, by vigil and pain,
Up with the sparrows among the spires.

For a man should live in a garret aloof,
And have few friends, and go poorly
    clad,
With an old hat stopping the chink in
    the roof,
To keep the Goddess constant and glad.

XXXV.

THE WORLD'S WAY.

At Haroun's court it chanced, upon a
time,
An Arab poet made this pleasant rhyme :

" The new moon is a horseshoe, wrought
of God,
Wherewith the Sultan's stallion shall be
shod."

On hearing this, his highness smiled,
and gave
The man a gold-piece. *Sing again, O
slave!*

Above his lute the happy singer bent,
And turned another gracious compli-
ment.

And, as before, the smiling Sultan gave
The man a sekkah. *Sing again, O
slave!*

Again the verse came, fluent as a rill
That wanders, silver-footed, down a
    hill.

The Sultan, listening, nodded as before,
Still gave the gold, and still demanded
    more.

The nimble fancy that had climbed so
    high
Grew weary with its climbing by and by:

Strange discords rose: the sense went
    quite amiss ;
The singer's rhymes refused to meet
    and kiss :

Invention flagged, the lute had got un-
    strung,
And twice he sang the song already
    sung.

The Sultan, furious, called a mute, and
    said,
O Musta, straightway whip me off
    his head!

Poets ! not in Arabia alone
You get beheaded when your skill is
    gone.

XXXVI.

PALINODE.

When I was young and light of heart
I made sad songs with easy art :
Now I am sad, and no more young,
My sorrow cannot find a tongue.

Pray, Muses, since I may not sing
Of Death or any grievous thing,
Teach me some joyous strain, that I
May mock my youth's hypocrisy !

XII SONNETS.

SONNETS.

"EVEN THIS WILL PASS AWAY."

Touched with the delicate green of early
    May,
Or later, when the rose unveils her face,
The world hangs glittering in star-
    strown space,
Fresh as a jewel found but yesterday.
And yet 't is very old ; what tongue may
    say
How old it is ? Race follows upon race·
Forgetting and forgotten ; in their place
Sink tower and temple ; nothing long
    may stay.
We build on tombs, and live our day,
    and die ;
From out our dust new towers and
    temples start ;
Our very name becomes a mystery.

What cities no man ever heard of lie
Under the glacier, in the mountain's
    heart,
In violet glooms beneath the moaning
    sea !

II.

AT STRATFORD-UPON-AVON.

Thus spake his dust (so seemed it as I
    read   ·
The words) : *Good frend, for Jesvs'
    sake forbeare*
(Poor ghost !) *To digg the dvst enclosèd
    heare —*
Then came the malediction on the head
Of who so dare disturb the sacred dead.
Outside the mavis whistled strong and
    clear
And, touched with the sweet glamour of
    the year,
The winding Avon murmured in its bed.
But in the solemn Stratford church the
    air
Was chill and dank, and on the foot-
    worn tomb
The evening shadows deepened mo-
    mently :
Then a great awe crept on me, standing
    there,

As if some speechless Presence in the
    gloom
Was hovering, and fain would speak
    with me.

III.

EGYPT.

Fantastic Sleep is busy with my eyes :
I seem in some waste solitude to stand
Once ruled of Cheops : upon either hand
A dark illimitable desert lies,
Sultry and still — a realm of mysteries :
A wide-browed Sphinx, half buried in
    the sand,
With orbless sockets stares across the
    land,
The woefulest thing beneath these
    brooding skies
Where all is woful, weird-lit vacancy.
'T is neither midnight, twilight, nor
    moonrise.
Lo ! while I gaze, beyond the vast sand-
    sea
The nebulous clouds are downward
    slowly drawn,
And one bleared star, faint-glimmering
    like a bee,
Is shut in the rosy outstretched hand of
    Dawn.

IV.

ENAMORED ARCHITECT OF AIRY RHYME.

Enamored architect of airy rhyme,
Build as thou wilt ; heed not what each
     man says.
Good souls, but innocent of dreamers'
     ways,
Will come, and marvel why thou wastest
     time ;
Others, beholding how thy turrets climb
'Twixt theirs and heaven, will hate thee
     all their days ;
But most beware of those who come to
     praise.
O Wondersmith, O worker in sublime
And heaven-sent dreams, let art be all
     in all ;
Build as thou wilt, unspoiled by praise
     or blame,
Build as thou wilt, and as thy light is
     given :
Then, if at last the airy structure fall,

Dissolve, and vanish — take thyself no
    shame.
They fail, and they alone, who have not
    striven.

6

v.

HENRY HOWARD BROWNELL.

They never crowned him, never knew
  his worth,
But let him go unlaureled to the grave :
Hereafter there are guerdons for the
  brave,
Roses for martyrs who wear thorns on
  earth,
Balms for bruised hearts that languish in
  the dearth
Of human love. So let the lilies wave
Above him, nameless. Little did he
  crave
Men's praises. Modestly, with kindly
  mirth,
Not sad nor bitter, he accepted fate —
Drank deep of life, knew books, and
  hearts of men,
Cities and camps, and war's immortal
  woe,
Yet bore through all (such virtue in him
  sate
His Spirit is not whiter now than then!)
A simple, loyal nature, pure as snow.

VI.

BARBERRIES.

In scarlet clusters o'er the gray stone-
　　wall
The barberries lean in thin autumnal
　　air :
Just when the fields and garden-plots are
　　bare,
And ere the green leaf takes the tint of
　　fall,
They come, to make the eye a festival !
Along the road, for miles, their torches
　　flare.
Ah, if your deep-sea coral were but rare
(The damask rose might envy it withal),
What bards had sung your praises long
　　ago,
Called you fine names in honey-worded
　　books —
The rosy tramps of turnpike and of lane,
September's blushes, Ceres' lips aglow,
Little-Red-Ridinghoods, for your sweet
　　looks ! —
But your plebeian beauty is in vain.

VII.

THE LORELEI.

Yonder we see it from the steamer's
    deck,
The haunted Mountain of the Lorelei —
The o'erhanging crags sharp-cut against
    a sky
Clear as a sapphire without flaw or fleck.
'T was here the Siren lay in wait to
    wreck
The fisher-lad. At dusk, as he passed
    by,
Perchance he 'd hear her tender, amor-
    ous sigh,
And, seeing the wondrous whiteness of
    her neck,
Perchance would halt, and lean towards
    the shore ;
Then she by that soft magic which she
    had
Would lure him, and in gossamers of her
    hair,
Gold upon gold, would wrap him o er
    and o'er,

Wrap him, and sing to him, and set him
  mad,
Then drag him down to no man knoweth
  where.

VIII.

TO L. T. IN FLORENCE.

You by the Arno shape your marble
      dream,
Under the cypress and the olive trees,
While I, this side the wild, wind-beaten
      seas,
Unrestful by the Charles's placid stream,
Long once again to catch the golden
      gleam
Of Brunelleschi's dome, and lounge at
      ease
In those pleached gardens and fair gal-
      leries.
And yet, perhaps, you envy me, and
      deem
My star the happier, since it holds me
      here.
Even so, one time, beneath the cypresses
My heart turned longingly across the
      sea,

Aching with love for thee, New England
    dear !
I would have given all Titian's god-
    desses
For one poor cowslip or anemone.

IX.

PURSUIT AND POSSESSION.

When I behold what pleasure is Pur-
    suit,
What life, what glorious eagerness it is ;
Then mark how full Possession falls from
    this,
How fairer seems the blossom than the
    fruit —
I am perplext, and often stricken mute
Wondering which attained the higher
    bliss,
The wingéd insect, or the chrysalis
It thrust aside with unreluctant foot.
Spirit of verse that still elud's ¡my art,
Thou airy phantom that dost ever haunt
    me,
O never, never rest upon my heart.
If when I have thee I shall little want
    thee !
Still flit away in moonlight, rain, and
    dew,
Wills-o'-the-wisp, that I may still pursue !

X.

THREE FLOWERS.

Herewith I send you three pressed with-
    ered flowers :
This one was white, with golden star ;
    this, blue
As Capri's cave ; that, purple and shot
    through
With sunset-orange. Where the Duomo
    towers
In diamond air, and under hanging bow-
    ers
The Arno glides, this faded violet grew
On Landor's grave ; from Landor's heart
    it drew
Its magic azure in the long spring hours.
Within the shadow of the Pyramid
Of Caius Cestius was the daisy found,
White as the soul of Keats in Paradise.
The pansy — there were hundreds of
    them, hid

In the thick grass that folded Shelley's
    mound,
Guarding his ashes with most lovely
    eyes.

XI.

AT BAY RIDGE, LONG ISLAND.

Pleasant it is to lie amid the grass
Under these shady locusts, half the day,
Watching the ships reflected on the Bay,
Topmast and shroud, as in a wizard's
     glass :
To see the happy-hearted martins pass,
Brushing the dewdrops from the lilac
     spray :
Or else to hang enamored o'er some lay
Of fairy regions : or to muse, alas !
On Dante, exiled, journeying outworn ;
On patient Milton's sorrowfulest eyes
Shut from the splendors of the Night
     and Morn :
To think that now, beneath the Italian
     skies,
In such clear air as this, by Tiber's
     wave,
Daisies are trembling over Keats's grave.

XII.

SLEEP.

When to soft Sleep we give ourselves
    away,
And in a dream as in a fairy bark
Drift on and on through the enchanted
    dark
To purple daybreak — little thought we
    pay
To that sweet bitter world we know by
    day.
We are clean quit of it, as is a lark
So high in heaven no human eye may
    mark
The thin swift pinion cleaving through
    the gray.
Till we awake ill fate can do no ill,
The resting heart shall not take up
    again
The heavy load that yet must make it
    bleed ;

For this brief space the loud world's
    voice is still,
No faintest echo of it brings us pain.
How will it be when we shall sleep in-
    deed ?